This
PJ BOOK
belongs to

_____

_____

PJ Library®

JEWISH BEDTIME STORIES and SONGS

A Note from PJ Library®

Helping Children Deal with Conflict

By virtue of living in the world, children will deal with conflict, within the family and with friends and classmates. With young children, issues might be a broken belonging, an unkind remark, or real or perceived unfairness or favoritism. With your help, your children can learn to deal positively and constructively with many different people and situations. Within families, the Jewish precept for getting along together is called "*shalom bayit*," peace in the home. Beyond our families, the imperative to act cooperatively is based on *v'ahavta l'rei'acha k'mocha*: you should love your neighbor as yourself -- which involves treating others as you would like to be treated.

- First, acknowledge to your children that they will come across difficult situations and people acting in ways that upset them.
- Discuss things that are necessary for a conflict to be resolved: an opportunity for each person to tell how s/he feels; a requirement that each person listen to the other's point of view; an attempt to understand the other's point of view; a desire to resolve the issue; a readiness to try the best solution offered.
- Children profit from repeated reminders that if they exhaust their own efforts to resolve a conflict, there are adults close by, ready to help them. Point to specific people your children know and can trust when they need help: parents, other adult family members, teachers, counselors, rabbis, physicians, etc.
- Children need opportunities to experience a wide variety of situations and "test" how to respond. Role-playing is an excellent way for children to do this, giving them a way to practice making sense of the world. As a family, brainstorm hypothetical situations and act them out, discussing feelings and reasoning.
- Remark on your children's ability to handle themselves well in difficult situations. Congratulate them when they are successful, pointing out specific behaviors that please you.

JEWISH BEDTIME STORIES and SONGS

www.**pjlibrary**.org

Snow in Jerusalem

The Old City

Muslim Quarter

Christian Quarter

Dome of the Rock

The Western Wall

David's Tower

Jewish Quarter

Al Aqsa Mosque

Armenian Quarter

Deborah da Costa

ILLUSTRATED BY

Cornelius Van Wright & Ying-Hwa Hu

ALBERT WHITMAN & COMPANY

CHICAGO, ILLINOIS

For my mother, who never saw Jerusalem,
and for Anthony, Danit, Stacey, and Warren, who did.
— D.D.

For Helene,
a true neighbor and a very good Samaritan.
— Y.H.H. & C.V.W.

With special thanks to Danit Clayman, Amy Littlesugar, Audrey Shabbas,
the Middle East Policy Council, Arab World and Islamic Resources and
School Services (AWAIR), and the Jewish Federation of Greater Washington
for stimulating interest and sharing expertise.

Also, thanks to Uri Yaffe of Jerusalem
for his photographs of the Old City.
— D.D.

*

Library of Congress Cataloging-in-Publication Data
da Costa, Deborah.
Snow in Jerusalem / by Deborah da Costa ;
illustrated by Cornelius Van Wright and Ying-Hwa Hu.
p. cm.
Summary: Although they live in different quarters of Jerusalem, a Jewish boy and a
Muslim boy are surprised to discover they have been caring for the same stray cat.
ISBN 978-0-8075-7525-3 (paperback)
[1. Cats — Fiction. 2. Snow — Fiction. 3. Jerusalem — Fiction.]
I. Van Wright, Cornelius, ill. II. Hu, Ying-Hwa, ill. III. Title.
PZ7.D122 Sn 2001   [E] — dc21   00-010204

The illustrations were rendered in watercolor and pencil on illustration board.
The display and text typeface is Quadraat.
The design is by Scott Piehl.

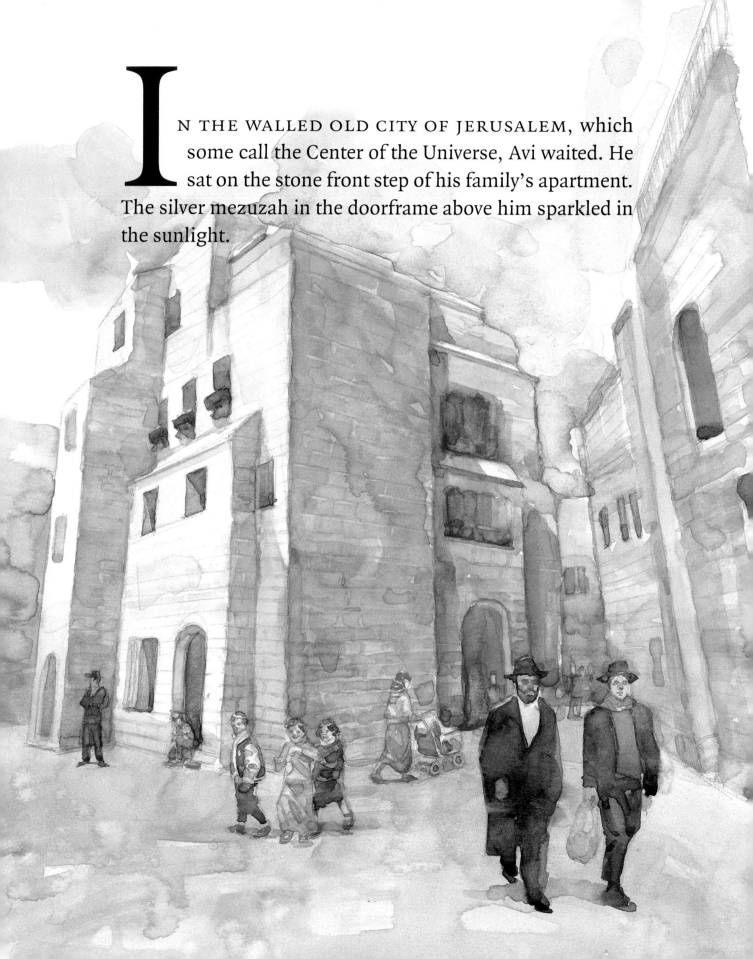

IN THE WALLED OLD CITY OF JERUSALEM, which some call the Center of the Universe, Avi waited. He sat on the stone front step of his family's apartment. The silver mezuzah in the doorframe above him sparkled in the sunlight.

Then he saw her, the small plump cat with long white fur.

"*Shalom* — hello — little cat," he said softly. "I have some warm chicken for you."

The cat purred as she ate. Then she rubbed against Avi's legs.

"Avi, my love, are you feeding that cat again?" his mother teased from the kitchen window. "We'll never get rid of it now!"

But Avi loved this fluffy white cat. "There is no other cat like you in all of Jerusalem," Avi whispered. "You are a miracle — a gift from Hashem, the Holy One."

The cat gazed at Avi with big eyes as clear and blue as the sea. "Mew," she said. Then she padded hastily down the wind-chilled street.

Avi watched, wondering where she was going. Suddenly he had an idea. "Cat," Avi called, "next time I will follow you!"

The cat moved through the winding streets of the Jewish Quarter. She ducked into shaded, cobbled alleyways and pranced through sunlit courtyards fragrant with the sweet smell of rosemary. Soon she reached the hustle and bustle of the Muslim Quarter.

Here the narrow streets were filled with shiny brass pots, colorful plates, and tapestries the color of fire.

Hamudi waited outside his family's small restaurant as the cat headed towards him.

"Ah, there you are, little white one. *Izz-ay-ik* — how are you?" Hamudi asked gently. He put down a plate of lamb and a bowl of water.

The cat purred as she ate and drank. Then she rubbed against Hamudi's legs.

"Hamudi, my darling, are you feeding the cat again?" his mother teased from the open doorway. "It will never leave us now!"

But Hamudi loved the silky white cat. "There is no other cat like you in all of Jerusalem," he whispered. "I know you must be a miracle — a gift from Allah!"

"Mew," the cat said. Then she padded off through the crowded streets.

Hamudi watched, wondering where she was going. Suddenly he had an idea. "Cat," he called, "next time I will follow you!"

But the next time did not come.

In the Jewish Quarter, Avi waited for many days. The cat was nowhere to be seen. There were many other cats, skinny cats with wild, hopeless eyes. They darted in and out of alleys and climbed on garbage bags. But not one of them was the beautiful white cat.

Avi worried.

And in the Muslim Quarter, Hamudi waited, too. Each day
he prepared the cat's favorite dish of lamb leftovers. But there
was no sign of her. There were many other cats. Big ones and
small ones. All had bony ribs and patchy fur. Not one of them
was the beautiful white cat.

Hamudi worried.

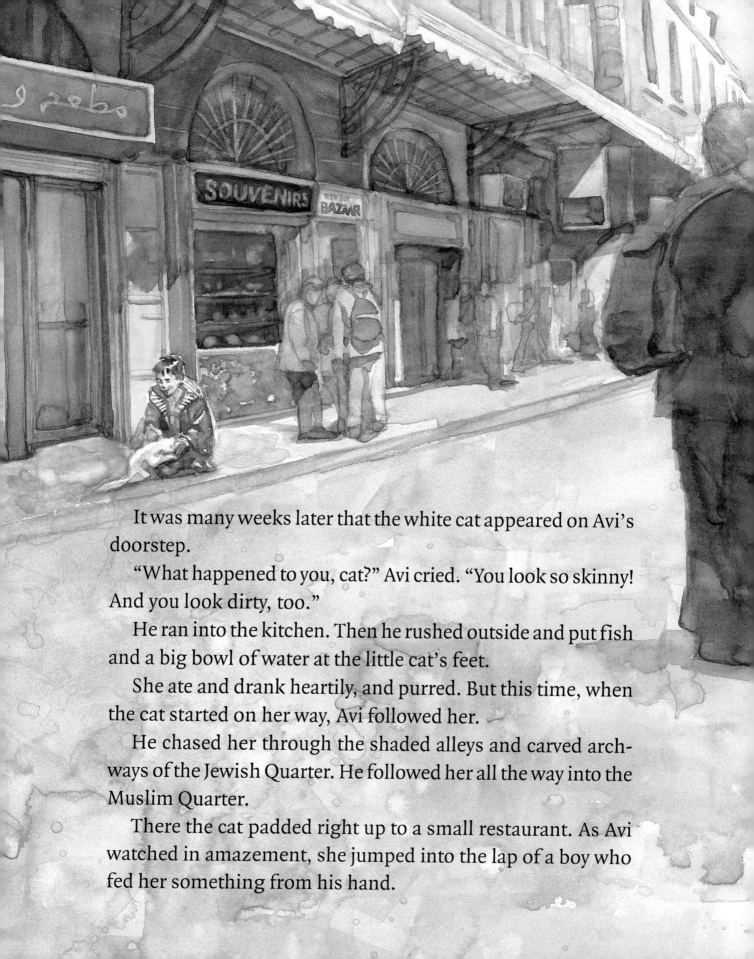

It was many weeks later that the white cat appeared on Avi's doorstep.

"What happened to you, cat?" Avi cried. "You look so skinny! And you look dirty, too."

He ran into the kitchen. Then he rushed outside and put fish and a big bowl of water at the little cat's feet.

She ate and drank heartily, and purred. But this time, when the cat started on her way, Avi followed her.

He chased her through the shaded alleys and carved archways of the Jewish Quarter. He followed her all the way into the Muslim Quarter.

There the cat padded right up to a small restaurant. As Avi watched in amazement, she jumped into the lap of a boy who fed her something from his hand.

Avi frowned. "That's my cat!" he shouted.

"Is not!" Hamudi yelled back. "She's *my* cat!"

The cat jumped out of Hamudi's lap and began running down the street.

"Now see what you've done!" Hamudi accused.

"Now see what *you've* done!" Avi answered back.

But just then something unusual happened. It began to snow in Jerusalem. Snowflakes floated gently through the air, swirling and twirling on their way to the earth.

The cat stopped for a moment and sat in the feathery whiteness. She sniffed at the crisp, cold air.

"My cat is getting all wet," Hamudi said.

"You mean *my* cat is getting wet. She could freeze in this weather!" Avi added.

Hamudi remembered how thin and scraggly the cat had seemed when she was in his lap. "We'd better help her, then," he said firmly.

The boys ran together. But the cat rounded the corner and disappeared into the streets of the Christian Quarter.

They tried to follow her paw tracks, but the spinning snow erased them faster than they could be found.

Side by side the two boys continued through the streets into the Armenian Quarter, catching glimpses of white fur through gusts of snow.

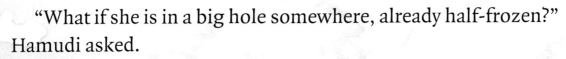

"What if she is in a big hole somewhere, already half-frozen?" Hamudi asked.

"Then we will warm her with our coats," Avi said.

But fear, like a dark cloud, began to follow them through the cold streets.

"*Chatul*, cat!" Avi sobbed in Hebrew. "*Chatul, chatul!*"

"*Ota*, cat!" Hamudi cried out in Arabic. "*Ota, ota!*"

The boys searched through street after street. Finally, they heard a faint sound like the muffled whine of the wind. They stopped and stepped closer to a darkened alley.

Hearing the sound again, Avi and Hamudi began to run, slipping and sliding on the snow-covered street. The cries were coming from some bags and cardboard cartons. The boys pushed them aside until they came to one small box. Curled inside was the white cat.

She was not half-frozen. And she was not alone.

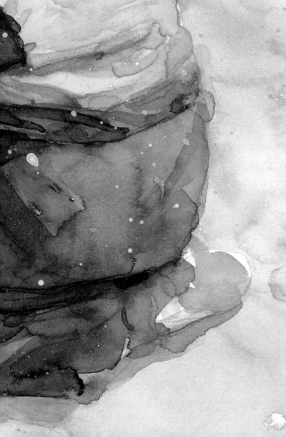

"It's a miracle," Avi said with a smile. "She has kittens — four of them!"

"Truly a miracle," Hamudi agreed, kneeling down to peer in the box.

Avi laughed. "No wonder the mama got so skinny!"

Hamudi nodded as he rubbed the fuzzy velvet tummy of one kitten.

"What will we do with all these cats?" Avi asked. "It's too dangerous for them to live outside in a box. They could freeze or be killed by mean dogs or bad people."

Hamudi thought about all the stray cats of Jerusalem with bony ribs and patchy fur. "We cannot just let them live on the streets."

"Then we must take them home," Avi told him.

"Yes," said Hamudi. "There's plenty of room at my house for five cats."

"Oh, no, no," Avi said quickly. "I saw the mother first.
So I get to take them home."
Hamudi scowled.
Silence crackled in the air between them.

Then Hamudi said sharply, "How do I know you saw the mother cat first? You can't prove it!"

"Neither can you!" Avi snapped back.

Leaving her kittens, the cat padded over to the spot where the boys stood arguing. She began to purr loudly and rub against the legs of each boy. Her tracks made a figure eight around them in the snow.

Avi bit his lip and looked away. "She does not want us to fight," he said slowly.

Hamudi stared down at his feet. "She wants peace."

"Then we will share," Avi said.

Hamudi smiled.

So the boys rummaged through the bags and cartons until they found two boxes that were just the right size. They put two kittens in each box.

"Who will get the mother cat?" Avi asked.

"I think she wants us to share her, too," Hamudi said with a grin.

"Yes," Avi agreed. "She can travel back and forth between us, the way she did before."

Then the two boys headed back to their homes in the Old City of Jerusalem, the place some call the Center of the Universe. With great care each boy carried two kittens in a small box. They were followed proudly by a blue-eyed white cat they named Snow.

AUTHOR'S NOTE

FOR CENTURIES JERUSALEM has been a holy place for Jews, Christians, and Muslims. It has been referred to as both the Center of the Universe and the Eternal City. Jerusalem has also been called the City of Peace despite the fact it has often been the object of bloody battles over religion and territory.

Today, Jerusalem is a city within a city. Surrounded by Arab East Jerusalem and Jewish West Jerusalem is the ancient Old City, an area of some 220 acres. The Old City is encircled by walls built in the sixteenth century by the Ottoman emperor Suleiman the Magnificent. Visitors may enter the Old City through one of seven large gates.

Inside, the Old City is divided physically and culturally into four sections: the Jewish Quarter, the Muslim (Arab) Quarter, the Armenian Quarter, and the Christian Quarter. These divisions are not totally segregated, however, and include some overlap of cultures. Nevertheless, Jewish and Arab children go to separate schools with Jews instructed in Hebrew and Arabs in Arabic. This creates an atmosphere of little social contact. Communication, if any, might be in English or simple Hebrew or Arabic.

Although the many cultures of Jerusalem live separate lives, they share the common experience of streets inhabited by many stray cats — cats that move easily through the quarters looking for food and shelter. So far, I have not seen a long-haired, blue-eyed, white cat in Jerusalem like the one in this story. But that does not mean such a cat does not exist. And on a rare snowy day in Jerusalem is waiting to inspire friendship and sharing.

GLOSSARY

ALLAH (al-LAH)
The word for God in Arabic.

ARAB
A cultural term referring to peoples originating in the
Arabian Peninsula who speak Arabic.

CHATUL (hah-TOOL)
The Hebrew word for cat.

HASHEM (hah-SHEM)
Refers to the God of the Jews, whose name is not spoken except in prayer.

HEBREW
Language of the Biblical Jews. Modern Hebrew
is the national language of Israel.

IZZ-AY-IK (Izz-AY-ick)
"How are you?" in Arabic.

MEZUZAH (muh-ZOO-zuh)
A small parchment scroll in a case containing passages from Deuteronomy.
It is attached to the right side of the doorframe as a sign of a Jewish home.

OTA (OH-tah)
The Arabic word for cat.

SHALOM (shah-LOHM)
A greeting in Hebrew. It means "hello," "goodbye," or "peace."
It is similar to the Arabic *salaam* (suh-LAHM).